This book belongs to

_____

WYNKEN, BLYNKEN, AND NOD

and Other Bed-Time Lullabies

Illustrated by

Bob Petillo

Poems by

EUGENE FIELD

The Unicorn Publishing House
New Jersey

Wynken,
Blynken
& Nod

Wynken, Blynken, and Nod one night
    Sailed off in a wooden shoe,—
Sailed on a river of crystal light
    Into a sea of dew.

"Where are you going, and what do you wish?"
    The old moon asked the three.
"We have come to fish for the herring fish
    That live in this beautiful sea;
    Nets of silver and gold have we!"
                Said Wynken,
                Blynken,
                And Nod.

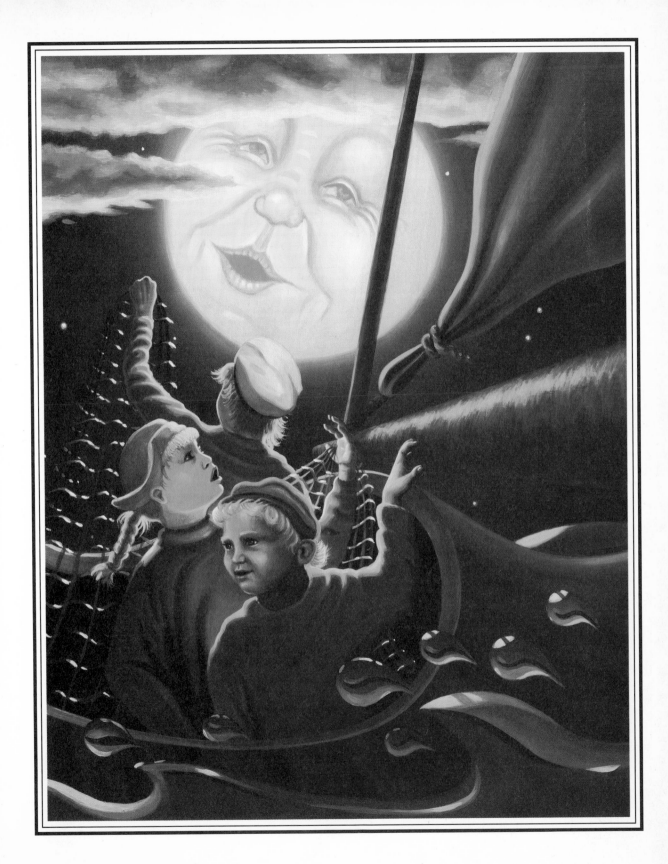

The old moon laughed and sang a song,
　　As they rocked in the wooden shoe;
And the wind that sped them all night long
　　Ruffled the waves of dew.
The little stars were the herring fish
　　That lived in that beautiful sea—
"Now cast your nets wherever you wish,—
　　Never afeard are we!"
　　So cried the stars to the fishermen three,
　　　　Wynken,
　　　　Blynken,
　　　　And Nod.

All night long their nets they threw
    To the stars in the twinkling foam,—
Then down from the skies came the wooden shoe,
    Bringing the fishermen home:
'Twas all so pretty a sail, it seemed
    As if it could not be;

And some folk thought 'twas a dream they'd dreamed
   Of sailing that beautiful sea;
   But I shall name you the fishermen three:
             Wynken,
             Blynken,
             And Nod.

Wynken and Blynken are two little eyes,
  And Nod is a little head,
And the wooden shoe that sailed the skies
  Is a wee one's trundle-bed;

So shut your eyes while Mother sings
   Of wonderful sights that be,
And you shall see the beautiful things
   As you rock in the misty sea
   Where the old shoe rocked the fishermen three:—
       Wynken,
          Blynken,
            And Nod.

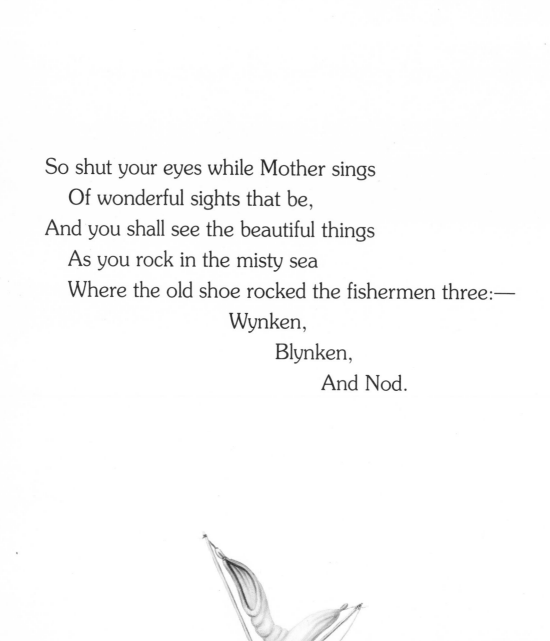

The Gingham Dog
and the Calico Cat

The gingham dog and the calico cat

Side by side on the table sat;

'Twas half-past twelve, and (what do you think!)

Nor one nor t'other had slept a wink!

    The old Dutch clock and the Chinese plate

    Appeared to know as sure as fate

There was going to be a terrible spat.

       (I wasn't there; I simply state

       What was told to me by the Chinese plate!)

The gingham dog went "bow-wow-wow!"
And the calico cat replied "mee-ow!"
The air was littered, an hour or so,
With bits of gingham and calico,
  While the old Dutch clock in the chimney-place
  Up with its hands before its face,
For it always dreaded a family row!
    (Now mind: I'm only telling you
    What the old Dutch clock declares is true!)

The Chinese plate looked very blue,
And wailed, "Oh, dear! what shall we do!"
But the gingham dog and the calico cat
Wallowed this way and tumbled that,
  Employing every tooth and claw
  In the awfullest way you ever saw—
And, oh! how the gingham and calico flew!
  (Don't fancy I exaggerate—
  I got my news from the Chinese plate!)

Next morning, where the two had sat
They found no trace of dog or cat;
And some folks think unto this day
That burglars stole that pair away!
But the truth about the cat and pup
Is this: they ate each other up!
Now what do you really think of that!
(The old Dutch clock it told me so,
And that is how I came to know.)

The Sugarplum Tree

Have you ever heard of the Sugarplum Tree?
  'Tis a marvel of great renown!
It blooms on the shore of the Lollipop Sea
  In the garden of Shut-Eye Town;
The fruit that it bears is so wondrously sweet
  (As those who have tasted it say)
That good little children have only to eat
  Of that fruit to be happy next day.

When you've got to the tree, you would have a hard time
    To capture the fruit which I sing;
The tree is so tall that no person could climb
    To the boughs where the sugarplums swing!
But up in that tree sits a chocolate cat,
    And a gingerbread dog prowls below—
And this is the way you contrive to get at
    Those sugarplums tempting you so:

You say but the word to that gingerbread dog
   And he barks with such terrible zest
That the chocolate cat is at once all agog,
   As her swelling proportions attest.
And the chocolate cat goes cavorting around
   From this leafy limb unto that,
And the sugarplums tumble, of course, to the ground—
   Hurrah for that chocolate cat!

There are marshmallows, gumdrops, and peppermint canes,
   With stripings of scarlet or gold,
And you carry away of the treasure that rains
   As much as your apron can hold!

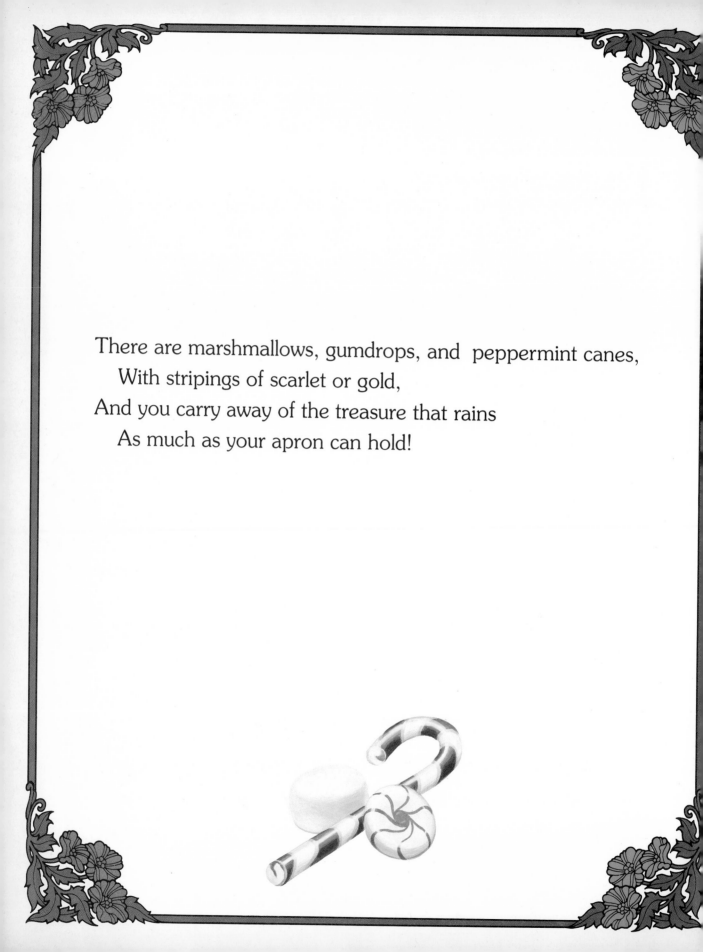

So come, little child, cuddle closer to me
    In your dainty white nightcap and gown,
And I'll rock you away to that Sugarplum Tree
    In the garden of Shut-Eye Town.

For over a decade, Unicorn has been
publishing richly illustrated editions of
classic and contemporary works for children
and adults. To continue this tradition,
WE WOULD LIKE TO KNOW WHAT YOU THINK.

If you would like to send us your suggestions or
obtain a list of our current titles, please write to:
THE UNICORN PUBLISHING HOUSE, INC.
P.O. Box 377
Morris Plains, NJ 07950
ATT: Dept CLP

Printing History 15 14 13 12 11 10 9 8 7 6

Library of Congress Cataloging-in-Publication Data

Field, Eugene, 1850-1895.
    Wynken, Blynken, and Nod / by Eugene Field ; illustrated by Bob Petillo.
p.cm.
    Summary: A collection of three of Field's story-poems, including "Wynken, Blynken, and Nod," "The
Gingham Dog and the Calico Cat," and "The Sugar Plum Tree."

    1. Children's Poetry, American. [1. American poetry.] I. Petillo, Bob, 1949-ill. II. Title.
PS1667.W8 1989
811'.4—dc20 89-4815
CIP   AC